Date Due

MARCOS

A MOUNTAIN BOY OF MEXICO

BY

MELICENT HUMASON LEE

PICTURES BY

BERTA AND ELMER HADER

JUNIOR PRESS BOOKS

ALBERT WHITMAN
& CO

CHICAGO

1937

ABOUT MARCOS

There is a story that is as old as the hills and as new as each day's sunrise. It is the backbone of folktale the world over, the story that never fails its listeners, and it begins: "There was a boy who set out to seek his fortune—"

To that brave and happy band of adventurers, an undaunted procession that winds from the first beginnings of story-telling down to the present day, Márcos belongs. He is one with all those boys who have set out, in many countries and by various roads, on the same quest. We see him against the bright sun-steeped landscape of Mexico, a small lonely figure, very much in earnest, rather bewildered at times, but never losing sight of his object — a job in the big city and, some day, the purchase of that fine yoke of oxen and the plow which he dreams of driving home so proudly to the little mountain village where he was born.

Simplicity is the essence of successful writing for children. In Márcos we find it combined with a somewhat rare quality, the ability to select out of a wealth of possible detail just what is essential to the story, and no more. There is no excess of description. What we see, we see through Márcos' own eyes and just as he saw it; the mountain trail, the friendly old goatherd, the village with its gay adobe houses, the potter and the basket-maker and the hurrying market folk all with the clear, direct vision of a little boy seeing these things, watching these people, for the first time. And through the whole story, like the threads which Márcos so loved and which led him at last to his desire, run the instinctive love of beauty and color, the craftsman's understanding of things shaped by hand, which are the heritage of every Mexican child.

It is good for children of all ages to learn how other children live, how other children work, the things they see and handle in daily life. In a day of constantly widening horizons the child's story book plays a very important part. It is the first step in travel, in the knowledge of other lands and customs. More and more of late years there has grown the need for stories of just this kind. Side by side with the many friends from far-off countries, from every corner of the world, to be met in the books and pictures of today Márcos will take his place in this growing saga of childhood.

Margery Bianco.

CONTENTS

Page

Márcos Leaves His Village 5

The Swinging Bridge of Vines 11

The Step in the Dark 17

Down in the Marshes 23

In the Hut of the Charcoal Burners 30

The Yellow Bowl and the Apple Sauce 37

The Soup Woman and the Centavos 45

The Lady in Lilac 54

The Old Convent 62

The Great City 70

Márcos Finds a Master 75

Spanish Words Used in This Story

Adiós (Ah-dee-ōs'), a word used in greeting or parting.
agave (ah-gah'-vay), wild century plant.
Arre (Ah'-rrray), Go on! A command to burros or oxen.
centavos (sen-tah'-vōs), copper pennies.
corredor (kōr-ray-dōr'), a veranda.
el tigre (el tee'-gray), a ring-tailed cat, or jaguar.
ex-convento (āx-kōn-ven'-tō), an old-time convent.
mozo (mō'-sō), a man servant.
Oaxaca (Wah-hah'-kah), a city in a state of the same name.
olla (oy'-yah), a clay jar.
Pasé! (Pah-say'!), Come in!
patio (pah'-tee-ō), courtyard of a house.
rebozo (ray-bō'-sō), a scarf worn by women.
señora (sayn-yōr'-ah), lady, Mrs.
serape (say-rah'-pay), a blanket.
serrano (say-rrrah'-nō), a mountaineer.
siesta (see-es'-tah), a rest in the middle of the day.
tortilla (tor-tee'-yah), flat, round, pancake-like bread.
Zapotec (Sah'-pō-tek), race of Indians in Oaxaca.

He peered out of the gray fringe of his serape.

I
Márcos Leaves His Village

EARLY dawn in the mountains. Early dawn in the little Zapotec Indian village hidden among the pine trees. Early dawn creeping into the tiny, thatched hut.

Márcos turned over on his mat of woven palm. Cold dawn touched his shoulder. He turned over again. Cold dawn met his face. And then he remembered!

This was the day he was going to the great city of Oaxaca to find work! This was the day he was going to leave his home.

He peered out of the gray fringe of his *serape,* or blanket. Dawn was creeping through the cracks between the cane stalks of which the little hut was built. Its silvery fingers touched the sleeping forms of his mother and father on their woven mat in their corner. They touched a cinnamon-colored hen in another corner, her feathers fluffed over her baby chicks. They touched a sleeping white goat in another corner.

Now the Indian boy rose stiffly, for the night had been cold on the mountain top. He stretched and stretched his legs and arms until he felt easy again.

Then he took his pointed hat from a peg and set it over his thick, black hair. He rolled up his sleeping mat and rain cape of palm into a snug bundle and slung them across his back. He folded up his gray *serape* and tossed it upon his shoulder.

Now he was ready for the trail. He glanced once more at his sleeping parents, and stole out of the door of the hut.

"I will not wake them," he said to himself, "for they are tired out from hoeing the cornfield yesterday, and they know that I must take the trail at dawn."

For just one moment Márcos stood before the hut and looked round at the little village he was going to leave. This was his home. He had never known another — he, a little *serrano*, a mountaineer. Many of the Zapotecs were *serranos*.

Where would he live in the great city? Would he lie down and sleep on his mat before the carved door of some rich man—guarding, always guarding, even though he slept? Would he crawl under the branches of a tree in a park and snooze at night, and in the daytime black the shoes of the Mexican gentlemen who sat on the fine benches of which his father had told him? Where would he live in the great city?

How friendly his village looked in the early light of dawn. Its little cane huts seemed as delicate as bird cages, but they were strong enough to shed mountain storms. The palm thatch which villagers had gathered from palm trees in a warm little canyon below, was as shaggy as the hair of his goat. The huts had no windows, because the sun could always creep through the cracks, and the smoke of the fire could always creep out.

Everybody was asleep. The dogs were out hunting rabbits in the wild mountain meadows beyond. So there was not even a dog's cold nose to nestle into his hand and bid him good-bye.

Márcos walked slowly toward the stone fence that hemmed in the village. He unlatched the gate, stepped out, and closed it again. And now he took the trail.

He had never followed this trail very far. He had often scrambled over the rocks beside it to herd the goats, or gone down into the meadow to hoe the corn. But he had gone only a little way along the trail itself. What would he find at the end? The great city, which his father had described to him so many times. Two days, three days, maybe, he would be on the trail before he reached it.

He took a hitch in the cord of his net so that his apples wouldn't bounce so much on his back, and rolled up his trousers to give his legs more freedom. Then down the trail he trudged.

His little black hat of rough felt looked like the hat of a gnome. It was pointed like a roof so that thunder showers in the summer rainy season — and now was the season — would slide off it. His cotton jacket and trousers, once white, were the color of mountain earth, and had been torn many times by brambles. Around his waist, under his coat, he wore a red cotton sash, the fringes of which dangled below the edge of his coat.

Down, down, down the trail he trudged under fragrant sprays of pine. He reached up and pulled off a handful of needles as he walked to sniff their perfume. How he loved these slender needles! If they were joined together what a long green string they would make!

At last he was out of sight of the village. He stopped a moment and stared at the scene before him. How big the world was! Far in the distance, farther than a bird would wish to fly without resting, he thought, rose three great, towering peaks. The rising sun was brushing them with pink color like the juice of wild berries. These mountains seemed to float before his eyes. They seemed alive and sparkling with hidden fires.

Far down in a canyon off the trail he saw the sun-dipped fronds of the palm trees where the *serranos* had gathered thatch for their huts. In another little canyon on the other side of the trail he saw a vivid green patch of cane, from which the huts were made.

He trudged on again, jouncing his net of apples into place. Down, down, down.

Suddenly he saw the face of an old Indian peering through the sprays of a pine tree. The Indian was crossing the boy's path. His pointed hat was rusty with age, and his gray *serape* was shabby and full of holes.

Márcos stopped short, and the two *serranos* stared at one another.

Then the old man spoke.

"Where are you going?"

"To the great city," said Márcos a little proudly, for this Indian looked as if he had never been to the great city.

The old man shook his head, and his hand trembled on his knotty pine stick.

"You will not find the city good, my son," said he. "There are too many people and not enough stars. The air is caught in an *olla* (a jar), and will not come out." He took off his rusty little hat and let the morning breeze ruffle his gray locks.

Márcos hung his head.

"Why do you go?" asked the old man.

"I am going to find work," said Márcos. "I want to work until I can save enough *centavos* to buy a pair of oxen for my father. A pair of oxen to plow the land, to raise corn, to make flour for *tortillas*."

"Ah-h-h!" said the old man. "I see. Oxen are good. Oxen are strong. Oxen plow well. Go to the city and earn the *centavos* for the oxen, and then come back to your village and help your father plow the corn fields."

"I shall come back," said Márcos, "and help my father plow the fields when the rains of the rainy season wet them. I will come back then. But there are many needs always, and I shall stay in the city in the dry season."

"Where are you going?"

"It is well," said the old man. "And now, what are you carrying in your net?" His worn old eyes peered over the boy's shoulder.

"Apples," said Márcos, "little green apples from the warm, sunny hillsides below our village. Some say that the Spaniards planted them somewhere near the city, and that their seeds blew up to our mountains. But I do not believe it. I think they are wild apples."

"So do I," said the old man. "They were here when I was a boy and when my father was a boy and when my grandfather was a boy. They are wild. But yours are better than those that grow near my village. Will you trade me some for a few *tortillas*?"

He plucked three of the thin, pancake-like wafers, the Mexican bread, out of his jacket, the two front ends of which he had tied together to make a blouse.

Márcos suddenly remembered that he had eaten no breakfast, and that he was hungry.

"I will trade with you," he said, and he gathered some apples out of his net and rolled them into a net which the old man held open. Then he took the *tortillas* eagerly, and set his strong white teeth into them. The edges of the *tortillas* were ragged, and there were holes in them, but that didn't matter. They were good and hearty and satisfied his morning hunger.

"Did you think you could go as far as the great city without food?" asked the old man.

Márcos flushed under his golden-brown skin.

"I hoped to trade my apples on the way," he said. But he didn't add that he hated to wake his sleeping mother to make *tortillas* in the early dawn, and there were none left from the night before.

"Ah, that is well," said the old man with a smile. "Trade for everything or pay for everything. Ask of no one. Do not be a beggar."

"I will never be that!" said Márcos stoutly. "Never!"

And so he parted with the old man, and each went his own way. The old one trudged slowly up a little goat path to milk his goat, and the young one trudged quickly down toward the great city. Down, down, down.

II

The Swinging Bridge of Vines

Now it was golden afternoon. Warmer and warmer it grew, as the trail wound into a valley. The fragrant pines were far away. Márcos felt homesick as he breathed deeply and no longer smelled them. Pines! He never thought he would be so far away from his pines!

Golden-green leaves of wild banana trees now swayed over his path, and ferns as lacy as feathery clouds on windy days, sprawled in the hollows nearby.

He left the trail, plunged down into a warm little canyon, and breathed the steaming odor of strange plants. A large white butterfly flitted like a ghost before his eyes, and he stopped short and stared at it. Was it a spirit? He had never seen such a great winged creature.

And even as he stared, the sun no longer glistened upon the white butterfly. A shadow floated over the little glade, a growl of thunder boomed through the silence, and soft, splashing raindrops fell.

"The thunder shower!" said Márcos to himself, unrolling his rain cape of palm ribbons as he spoke. He shook out the folds and threw the cape around his shoulders. Then he pulled his funny black cap over his eyes, and ran into the thickest part of the banana jungle.

Under a roof of wide, drooping banana leaves he stood, while the rain splashed, the thunder rolled, and the lightning wove its shining thread of gold through the trees.

As the rain grew into a steady hum, the boy peered up into the tree above him. He spied a cluster of bananas, and he reached up and pulled one down. It had a thick, woody taste, but he liked it. He was very hungry now after his long tramp. He reached up and pulled down another and ate it. Then another.

"These bananas will keep me from hunger until nightfall," he murmured to himself, "and then — who knows? Perhaps I can trade a few of my apples for food and shelter in some hut. Perhaps I will lie down hungry in some little hollow."

He could not eat his apples because they were green and hard. They needed cooking, and he had no matches.

At the thought of going to sleep hungry he tied the front ends of his jacket into a blouse, just as the old man had done. He stuffed a few bananas into this blouse, so that he stuck out like a fat, little, cooking *olla*.

"Now I have enough food for two days, anyway," Márcos said to himself. And as he spoke, he felt a warm ray of sunlight on his cheek, and he looked up through the banana leaves and saw that the thunder storm had stopped. It had stopped almost as suddenly as it began.

He rolled up his rain cape, plunged up the slope of the warm little canyon again, crossed over to the trail and peered before him.

The shadows on the towering mountains far beyond were the color of wild grapes, and long chocolate shadows lay across the dusty trail. Late afternoon had slipped into the mountains while he was waiting in the rain under the banana trees. He must hurry if he would find a shelter before nightfall. He ran along the trail, crossed a meadow, and climbed a mountain slope that grew steeper and steeper and steeper. And then —

He stopped on the mountain crest and stared. Under his

He reached up and pulled one down.

pointed, black hat his dark eyes shone wide. One lock of black hair curled around his cheek like a horn. His chest rose and fell quickly under his dusty jacket.

He was staring at a deep, wide canyon that divided this mountain from the mountain beyond. Steep, jagged rocks faced each mountain. And far down in the hollow between these rocks ran a river that looked like a thread of blue yarn that a magician had touched into life.

But that was not all. Hung from mountain side to mountain side was a swinging bridge of vines! It looked as frail as a spider's web, as it glistened in the setting sun. It dipped 'way down in the center.

How could Márcos have forgotten this swinging bridge? His mother and father had often spoken of it. But somehow, it had seemed to him more like a dream-bridge than a real bridge. It seemed to belong to the old folk tales which his father was always telling him.

It seemed to belong to the stories of the Zapotecs, his people, fleeing from the Spaniards, their conquerors — the *serrano* Zapotecs in the mountains, and the lowland Zapotecs below. It had never seemed real to him, somehow. But now he would have to cross it.

Slowly he wove his way down among the rocks of the bank until he stood just opposite the swinging bridge of vines. Right across the chasm it stretched, quiet now that no footstep was upon it.

The boy remembered a story that his father told him one day. An old woman of the tribe was afraid to cross the bridge, and one of the men blindfolded her with his red cotton sash, so that she could not see the water far below. Then she crossed easily. But one man walked before her and one behind.

Márcos shut his eyes. His heart beat like the click of the wooden looms that wove the cotton sashes at home. He looked back toward the trail over which he had come. Would he have to turn back?

"There is no one to blindfold me with his sash," he thought. "Shall I blindfold myself? That would not be wise, for there is no one to walk before me, and no one to walk behind me. No one! No one! Not even the old man of the *tortillas*." He thought a long moment. "Shall I go back?"

And then he laughed aloud and faced the bridge again. "Am I

an old woman?" he asked himself. "Am I scared of a vine bridge which my father and mother have crossed for many moons? Which all of my people have crossed for many moons? If this vine bridge holds others it will hold me. How can I reach the great city unless I cross this bridge? It will always stand between me and the great city."

If he ever earned enough *centavos* to buy a pair of oxen he would have to drive them through the bed of the river in the dry season.

Now bravely he set one dusty brown foot on the bridge and clasped the vine rail with one hand. The bridge swayed like a spider web in the wind. He shut his eyes very tight, then he opened them wide again. He took one step forward, and then another, and then another. Soon he was walking softly and slowly in the very middle of the bridge.

He kept his eyes on the mountain before him. "I mustn't look down!" he thought, but it seemed as if he must look down. A voice in the river seemed to be calling, "Look down! Look down!"

And then Márcos laughed aloud again. "You can't fool me, old river! I won't look down — but even if I did, you wouldn't make me dizzy! This is the bridge of my people and I am at home on you!"

And so he crossed the bridge of vines for the first time, and he felt ashamed that he had been afraid of such a natural and beautiful thing.

Vines — vines woven together into such strength! Vines of his own mountains. Tiny threads woven into a strong sash as the threads of his cotton sash had been woven! He was proud of the vines of his mountains.

As he walked up the rocks on the opposite mountain he plucked another banana out of his blouse, and set his white teeth into the firm flesh of it.

"Ha-ha!" he chuckled. "I have done the hardest thing first. Now things will not seem so hard in the great city."

But as he scrambled over the rocks at the mountain's crest, he didn't know that the face of an old man was peering at him around the shoulder of another mountain peak.

For the old man of the *tortillas* had not found his goat where he had tied her. She had broken away from her rope, and had leaped up the rocky side of a mountain near by, and the old man had seen her laughing at him from the top of a peak.

Up and up he had followed her and caught her, and while he was leading her down from her perch, he had spied the old-time swinging bridge below. At the near end of the bridge was his new friend Márcos, his face turned away from the bridge, turned toward the homeward trail.

And the old man had said softly, just as if Márcos were listening to him:

"Cross the bridge, my little friend. Many bridges will you find to cross, and you can never go anywhere unless you cross a bridge. There will be bridges of toil and bridges of sorrow and bridges of pain. Cross the bridge!"

And just at that moment, Márcos had faced about again and stepped upon the bridge that led to the great city!

III

The Step in the Dark

It was almost dusk when Márcos saw a little village on a hill. The huts were built of carrizo cane and thatched with tules from the marshes, and they had only one door and no windows. He ran up a little path and peered over the stone wall.

Nobody seemed to live in the village at all. Nobody sat in the doorways or walked up and down the little paths. He peered closer, and saw threads of smoke squeezing through the chinks between the canes, and he said to himself:

"They are all inside their little huts eating their supper, while I stand outside cold and hungry."

He looked over his shoulder at his net of apples.

"I will trade some of my apples for a night's lodging and a good warm supper," he said to himself. "I will not have to eat just bananas."

So thinking, he pushed open the little gate and stepped into the village. No one ran out to meet him, and why should they? This was not his home. He had no companions here that he knew.

He walked up one little path that led to a hut on a knoll. This hut smelled good. It smelled of wet tules on the roof — wet from the thunder shower. It smelled of chicken feathers. It smelled of savory cooking.

Just behind this hut was a smaller hut that seemed to belong to it. Who could be living in that other hut? Why did these people need more than one house? Márcos was wondering about all these things as he peered into the doorway.

A cozy scene met his curious eyes. An old woman was sitting on the ground by a glowing fire, flipping over a *tortilla* on a clay cooking plate. A bowl of stew simmered over the fire. Over the old woman's lap skittered fluffy baby chicks of bright yellow, searching for the seeds that she had just flung out.

"Those baby chicks are safe for the night," thought Márcos. "Where is the mother hen, I wonder?"

In a corner near the old woman he saw the mother hen, blinking at him with angry eyes.

"Do not be afraid, little mother," thought Márcos. "I won't hurt you. I want shelter just as much as you do."

Just then the old woman looked up and saw him standing there. "*Paddy-ooch'-ee,*" she said, in the native tongue of the *serranos*. "Good day. What do you wish? A basket?"

"A basket?" Márcos stared. He didn't see any baskets.

The old woman saw his surprise, for her eyes always saw everything — every flicker, every frown on a face.

"You are in the house of Antonio, the basket maker," she said, "but he has gone to the city with baskets to sell, and he will not return until dawn, I think. I am his aunt. I live here and cook his *tortillas*. Why do you come?"

At the word *tortillas*, Márcos remembered why he came.

"I want to trade some of my green apples for supper and shelter for the night," he said. "They make fine apple sauce."

"Supper and lodging you shall have," said the old woman.

"Pour some of your apples in here." And she held out a brown clay dish.

The apples rattled into it as Márcos poured. He gave her a fair lot of them. Then his eyes glanced at the *tortillas* and the stew.

"Sit down," said the old woman. Márcos sat down on the earth beside her, and they ate a cozy little supper by the fire — the old woman and the boy.

When they had supped well, the old woman spoke:

"The lids are pulling down over your eyes and your head nods. I will show you where you can sleep. I am glad that you have come tonight, because I do not like to be alone."

"But you are not alone," said Márcos, nodding his head toward the other huts which he knew circled them in the dusk outside.

"One can be alone in the midst of others," muttered the old woman. "I do not like to have the baskets unguarded. Antonio always sleeps beside them."

"But who in the village would steal — " began Márcos.

"Hush!" warned the old woman. "Do not think thoughts like those, else they will come true." She lighted a fire brand as she spoke.

She led Márcos out the door, around the hut, and into the little hut in back of the other.

"Ah!" thought Márcos. "Now I know why these people have two houses. One of them is the house of baskets."

The old woman held the fire brand in the doorway of the basket hut. Márcos opened his dark eyes very wide. He had never seen so many baskets. They were all stacked one within the other, and they reached to the rafters above.

Very deep baskets they were — burro-baskets, for burros to carry. Márcos had often seen his people bring home these baskets, but he had never seen a basket house before.

"Unroll your mat in this corner," said the old woman, pointing to a clean corner where no baskets were piled. "This is where Antonio sleeps when he is home."

While Márcos was unrolling his mat, the old woman slipped away, and the hut was left in darkness.

"I am taking Antonio's place," thought Márcos, as he rolled himself up in his warm *serape*. "I must keep one eye open while I sleep." But how could he do that?

Already he had shut both eyes, and he fell into a deep, deep sleep. A little scratching sound woke him up. He sat up straight and listened. Then he lay down again.

"I know that sound," he mumbled to himself. "It is a little mouse. She is chewing one of Antonio's baskets." Many and many a time had he heard the scratching and chewing and thumping of mice in the little hut at home.

He closed his eyes and slept again. A second time he sat up straight. He listened. He certainly heard something different now. He strained his ears until he thought they were going to burst. He wished they were as wide as a burro's ears.

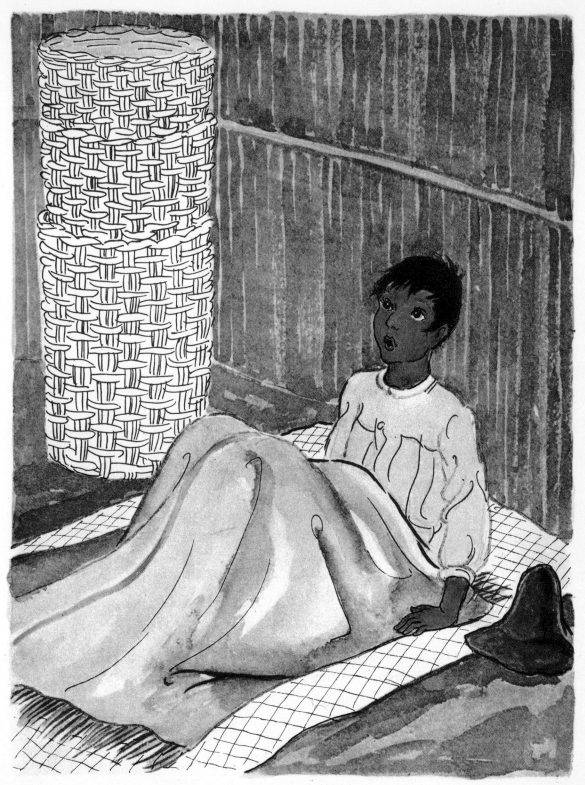

He sat up straight and listened.

He heard stealthy footsteps creeping up to the door. Moonbeams shone on a dark hand touching the door frame. A shadowy form, a dark something in another hand, and then —

Márcos leapt to his feet. The thief was going to throw the baskets into that dark blanket he held, and glide away. Márcos tore the blanket from the dusky hand.

"Out of here — out!" he cried, in a choking voice.

Silence, and then a low chuckle. "Is that the way you greet an old woman who wants to give you a warmer cover this cold night? There has been no fire in the basket house, and —"

"Oh!" whispered Márcos. "I thought, I thought —"

"I know what you thought," chuckled the old woman. "You thought someone was going to steal Antonio's baskets, and you thought we could trace him by the blanket that you were going to snatch. I wish that you lived here all the time, Antonio goes away so often. But now, wrap yourself in that blanket and sleep, for it is still a long time until dawn." And she stole away.

Márcos smiled to himself in the dark. He wished that he lived here, too. He would gather faggots for the old woman's fire; he would help Antonio cut the canes for his baskets; he would learn the basket trade. And when Antonio went away to the great city, he would sleep in the basket house and guard the baskets. Never would he let anyone steal them.

Then a thought choked him. "The great city! I must go to the great city. Shall I find kind old women there who will cook my supper? Who will think of me on cold nights and bring me warm blankets? Shall I sleep in some cozy corner of a basket house, or in the cold doorway of a stranger's house?"

So thinking, he fell asleep, and he dreamed that the great city was built of baskets. The walls were woven of carrizo canes like the walls of the baskets, and they were as high as the mountains that circled his own village. And through their chinks drifted the smoke of supper fires.

And as he slept, the little mouse chewed a hole in one of Antonio's baskets, where tiny, fragrant seeds from the tule marshes had clung to the tule basket rim.

IV

Down in the Marshes

While Márcos was eating his breakfast of stew and *tortillas* with the old woman, she said:

"Antonio came back in the early dawn, while you were still asleep. He peeked into the basket hut and saw you, but he did not wake you."

"Where is he now?" asked Márcos, taking another bite into his *tortilla*.

"He is cutting canes in the marshes," said the old woman. "Canes for his new baskets."

"And I will cut canes, too," said Márcos, wiping his mouth with the back of his little brown hand. "This is a good breakfast and I wish to earn it."

"Cut canes then," said the old woman. "It is well. Antonio never has enough help." She rose and drew a very large knife from the thatched wall of the hut.

Márcos took the knife and looked out of the little doorway. He saw many other huts snuggled about him, the smoke from breakfast fires oozing through their walls. He saw Indian women gathering faggots, or bearing water jars on their heads, on their way to the spring. He saw Indian men feeding and watering their burros.

Now he ran out of the hut, down a hill, and into the marshes at the back of the village. Green and inviting rose the fringe of cane along the marshes. Already the boy could smell its freshness. Among the long curling leaves he saw the figure of a man in white coat and trousers.

Márcos ran quickly until he set foot in the moist marshes, then shyness tugged him back. He stood silently in the wet sand.

Clack, clack! rang the sound of the breaking canes as the knife swished through them and cut them down to the earth. Cane upon cane swished down. Their free, growing life in the marshes was over now. They were almost ready to be woven into baskets. Soon they would be ready for their trip to market on the sides of a burro.

He saw Indian women bearing water jars on their heads.

The clacking stopped. The man raised his hand to wipe off the sweat from his forehead. He turned. He saw Márcos.

"Ho!" he chuckled. "You are the boy who guarded my baskets last night. And did a thief steal some of them in a blanket?"

Márcos flushed under his dark skin. He wished he had not come to help this man. He stood ready to fly toward the hut.

"But you made my old aunt glad," said the other quickly, seeing that he had hurt the boy's feelings. "She is afraid to stay alone. She does not like to have me go to the city. Do you want to help me cut canes?" He had seen the knife in the boy's hand.

Márcos stepped toward him. "I want to help you cut canes to pay for my breakfast," he said simply.

"Canes you shall cut," said Antonio. "I often wish I had a strong boy like you to cut my canes. Then I would have only to weave my baskets."

"There it is again!" thought Márcos. "A chance to stay here and earn my meals and lodging. But how could I ever earn enough to buy a pair of oxen? And that is what my father wants me to do! No — I will go on to the great city. I must!"

And as if he knew what the boy was thinking, Antonio said:

"Are you going to the city?"

"Ay, to the great city," said Márcos, and his heart felt as heavy as though a load of tiles was fastened to it. He smelled again the freshness of the cane; he felt the cool wet sand between his toes; he heard the gentle rustle of the cane leaves. What sights and sounds and smells would there be in the great city?

"And why are you going there?" asked Antonio, as the two of them drove their knives through the base of the canes, and the canes fell with a soft swish on the earth.

"To buy an oxen and a plow for my father," said Márcos.

Cla-a-ack! Cla-a-ack! Swish! More canes were cut; more canes fell.

Then Antonio said half aloud, half to himself:

"Some there are who like to plow, and some who like to sow, but it seems to me that the weaving of a basket is best."

As he spoke, Márcos was resting a little moment, and shredding a cane leaf between his pointed fingers. He thought to himself:

"This leaf is woven of tiny threads. Strong threads. Threads like those in the bridge of vines."

Again he cut a cane with a cla-a-ack, and again it fell with a swish to the ground.

When many canes were cut, the two of them tied them in bundles and threw the bundles over their shoulders. They plodded up the hill. The old woman was waiting for them at the back of the hut.

"We will show the boy how to make a basket," she chuckled. "I know he doesn't want to go away yet."

Márcos smiled. He felt as if he didn't want to go away, ever.

On the ground near him lay the round unfinished base of a large burro basket. It was shaped like the spokes of a wheel, the split canes sticking out all round from the center. When the base was finished, thought Márcos, the canes would be bent up straight to make the sides.

Antonio and Márcos laid the canes near the basket-base, and Antonio and his old aunt sat down beside them. Márcos squatted down, too, and watched them carefully.

Antonio took his long knife, scraped off the heavy husks of canes and stripped off the crackling leaves. Blood oozed from the side of his finger, because the edge of the husk was very sharp. Then he quickly scraped off the knots in the joints of the cane.

The old woman took her knife from Márcos, and split the canes into slender strips. Now they were ready for the weaving.

Then while the old woman was still splitting more and more canes, Antonio took up a slender strip and wove it so swiftly in and out the basket canes that Márcos could hardly see what he was doing. The circle of the base grew wider and wider, and soon Antonio would bend up the canes and weave the sides.

As Márcos stood there watching, he heard the creak of an ox cart in the fields beyond, and saw two creamy oxen trudging across the freshly plowed field. He heard the cry of the ox driver, *"Arre! Arre!* Go on! Go on!"

And then he remembered his errand to the great city, and the task that was before him, and he thought to himself:

And so he bade them "Adiós."

"I gave apples to the old woman for my supper and shelter, and I cut canes for my breakfast. Now I can go."

"Going, eh?" asked Antonio, guessing his thoughts. "You have a long way ahead of you." He swiftly wove a fresh strip of cane into the basket.

"Ay, a long way," said the old woman, shaking her head.

"But oxen are at the end of it," said Antonio, weaving another strand over and under. "And may they be good and strong!"

"The ones I choose will be good and strong!" said Márcos. He ran into the basket hut, wrapped up his palm mat and rain cape, and flung them upon his shoulder with his *serape* and apple net.

And so he bade them *"Adiós,"* and trudged down the hill into the trail again.

As he drifted out of sight around a curve, the old woman said to her nephew:

"Ah! You were a boy like that, Antonio, with your eyes always facing ahead. When you were a tiny lad you used to run to the marshes and cut little strips off the canes and weave tiny baskets for the little burro that you made out of clay. And you would fill your baskets with little balls that you called pottery. Ah, well I remember that. And now you have a basket house, and your baskets are the best and finest in the great city." She smiled proudly.

"Ay!" sighed Antonio. "I always wanted to make baskets. I never cared about the plowing and sowing. And I do not think that this boy cares just for those, either. That is his father's wish. It is not his. He has his own wish."

"And what is it?" asked the old woman curiously.

"I do not quite know," said Antonio slowly. "I do not think it is his wish to make baskets, though he seemed to like the cutting of the canes. I think—" And then he shook his head. "I do not know. I do not think he knows, yet."

And as Márcos trudged along the trail, he thought to himself:

"I wish I didn't have to go away from those good people. I liked the rustle of the cane leaves."

V

In the Hut of the Charcoal Burners

It was dusk again when Márcos spied a few huts on a hill top. They were perched like goats among the rocks. The lower half of them was built of stone, and the upper half of adobe, or sun-dried bricks. The adobe was not painted over, so it was just the color of the mud from which it was made. A heavy thatch of palm leaves, like bushy eyebrows, roofed the huts.

Near one of the houses a strong tall Indian was unloading a burro, and a little girl was carrying a bundle of faggots toward a doorway.

"Ho!" thought Márcos. "Now I can trade some of my apples for supper and lodging. Bananas they have plenty, for warm canyons lie all around them."

He left the trail and stepped up a little goat path which led toward the huts. As his shadowy figure loomed nearer the stone fence which hemmed them in, a bunch of dogs rushed out of the open gate, snarling and yapping. Their lips were drawn back from their ugly teeth.

"Hey!" growled the strong tall man in a voice of thunder. "Come back here!" The dogs tucked their tails between their legs and shrank back.

The Indian stepped to the gate, and the little girl followed him, clutching her faggots and staring and staring.

"What do you want?" asked he, as Márcos trudged up to the gate. The man's face was stained with black smudges.

"I have apples to trade for my supper and lodging," said Márcos, jerking his head toward the net which hung over his shoulder. "Will you trade?"

"Ay!" said the man, peering at him closely. "Come in."

Márcos entered the gateway and the Indian closed the gate, leaving the dogs outside. Now he was already snug and safe in this little cluster of huts.

Without a word the tall Indian led the way up a little rise to his own hut. Márcos glanced about him. He saw empty blackened nets lying on the ground by the burro, and he knew that they had been filled with charcoal. Márcos guessed that the man had just returned from the great city below, where he had sold charcoal to the housewives. The boy smelled charcoal burning somewhere in the pits. Ah! These were huts of charcoal burners.

He followed the tall man into the little doorway. It was dusky in the hut except for the glow of a fire in the center of the earth floor. Sitting by the fire was a youngish woman stirring goat stew in a brown clay *olla*. The fumes from the stew mingled with the smell of charcoal which clung to the rafters of the hut. A fresh bundle of faggots was lying by the fire—the faggots that the little girl had been carrying.

"She is somewhere in the hut now," thought Márcos, and he peered into the dusky shadows of every corner. She was crouching in one of them like a scared rabbit.

The man uttered a few words to the woman. She picked up a fresh wad of dough which lay on a clay dish beside her, and patted it into a *tortilla*, flinging it from palm to palm of her hands. Clip, clop, clip, clop, sounded her patting through the tiny hut. She tossed the *tortilla* down upon a shallow plate over the fire. Then clip, clop, clip, clop again. She was making another *tortilla*. She started to turn over the first *tortilla* with her fingertips. It stuck.

"Ah!" she grunted. "Gloria, come here! Grind me more chalk for my plate."

The little girl crept shyly out of her corner, picked up a rock and

Márcos and the little family squatted around the blaze.

pounded into powder some white chalk that lay upon a stone slab. The woman scraped the cooking plate clean, powdered it with the chalk, and tossed another *tortilla* upon it.

Soon supper was ready. Márcos and the little family squatted around the blaze and held out their clay dishes to the woman. She filled them with good goat stew and handed them each *tortillas*. They folded their *tortillas* into little scoops, dished up the stew with them, and then ate their *tortilla* scoops, too. They sucked heartily and licked their fingers.

The night wind rose and blew around the hut, and Márcos was glad that he was snug and cozy within friendly walls. He was glad he was not trying to keep warm in some damp little hollow.

Clip, clop, clip, clop — more *tortillas*. Swish — as the wooden spoon ladled out more stew. And always the sighing wind.

Then the man spoke to Márcos:

"Where are you going?"

"To the great city," said Márcos.

"What are you going to do there?"

"Work," said Márcos. But even as he spoke his heart grew as heavy as a bag of stones, because he did not know what work he would find.

But the man said simply:

"Ay, you will find work. You are young and strong." But he did not say aloud what he added to himself, "And you have a pleasant way with you."

The woman pointed to the apples and chuckled. Márcos gathered handfuls of them and poured them into a bowl which she held out. He filled the bowl. Two or three apples rolled out, and the little girl caught one and set her teeth into it. But the woman snatched it away from her.

"No, no! It must be cooked first," she said.

Now they all sat gazing into the fire, for they were too drowsy to talk. Once the little girl rose secretly and stole across the earth floor of the hut. She opened the door a crack and peered out.

"Hey!" cried her father. "Come back!" She crept back and nestled by her mother.

"She lost a little kid today," said her father. "She has been hunting for it all the afternoon, so her mother tells me."

"Ay," said the mother. "It strayed away, and it is not with the flock tonight. They are all safe in the corral but that little one."

The child began to softly weep at her words.

"She is afraid that *el tigre*, the ring-tailed jaguar, will catch it," said the father.

The little girl sobbed louder.

"Hush! Hush!" crooned her mother. "It cannot be helped."

The wind roared around the hut. The father and mother and the little girl wrapped their *serapes* around them, and curled down to sleep upon a palm-woven mat. Márcos unrolled his own little mat and spread it in a corner. He folded his *serape* closely around him, too, and nestled down. The fringe tickled his lips and he turned it inside.

He folded his serape closely around him.

Now they were all asleep but Márcos. He could hear the rise and fall of their breathing—even the breathing of the little girl. The wind howled and howled outside, but it was warm inside the hut. It was warm and snug inside, and yet . . . Outside, somewhere, a little kid was alone. Caught in the rocks, perhaps. She would be bleating softly somewhere. And the black and yellow *tigre* would hear that bleating.

Silently Márcos arose. Silently he folded the *serape* closer around him. He tiptoed across the earth floor of the hut. He pushed open the door. Darkness and many stars. He remembered what the old man had told him:

"There are too many people in the city and not enough stars."

He crept down to the gate, unlatched it, and stole out into the night. He listened. The dogs were hunting, he guessed. Perhaps they were far away. Surely one dog was lying in the corral with the sheep, in back of the hut somewhere.

He walked farther and farther, feeling his way with his bare toes. He listened. He heard nothing but the sighing of the wind. He walked a little farther, his eyes growing more and more used to the dark. Now he could see where he was stepping. He listened. This time he heard a faint bleating. Ah! The little kid.

He ran now. He ran to a loose cluster of gray rocks looming up in the starlight like crouched Indians wrapped in their *serapes*. He lightly ran up one rock. He glanced quickly about him. In a little hollow underneath a rock shelf he spied a trembling blob of white.

The little kid had fallen into that twisty cave, and could not find her way out. She had been bleating all the afternoon, thought the boy, but her bleating was muffled under the rocks. But Márcos had the ears of a *tigre* itself.

He slid down, gathered the trembling little creature in his arms, wrapped it in his warm *serape,* and carried it to the hut. How fine and silky its hair felt. As soft as corn silk, as soft as pine needles. He lifted it tenderly over the corral to the flock below. It ran to its mother.

Then Márcos stole to the door of the hut, slipped in, lay down on his mat and wrapped his *serape* closely around him. He slept.

And in the morning the little girl found the kid snug and safe in the corral with all the others.

VI

The Yellow Bowl and the Apple Sauce

Márcos left the charcoal hut early in the morning. His jacket-blouse was stuffed with a few bananas, and a chunk of mutton and some *tortillas* which the wife of the charcoal burner had given to him. His net was still two-thirds full of his green mountain apples. He felt very rich.

A good breakfast inside of him, a good supper for the night, and apples to trade. What could be better?

He was traveling between rolling hills now, soft hills furred in green, and the path was gentle. Up a little way, down a little way, but always easy and always going down more than up.

Many Indians flocked into the trail from tiny villages hidden among the hills. They were not *serranos*. They were lowland Indians. The men wore wide-brimmed hats of woven palm, and their white cotton jackets and trousers were clean. The women were daintily dressed in white blouses with tiny puffed sleeves, bright skirts with flounces, and blue *rebozos* or scarves over their heads.

Many of the Indians were trotting along with quick, short steps; many were riding their fuzzy burros; many were jouncing along in ox carts. Wider and wider grew the trail.

It seemed friendly and pleasant to Márcos to have so many Indians near him, and yet the boy felt timid, also. Too many people and not enough stars. Well, there were not too many people yet. There were just enough to be interesting. He liked to watch them.

Only once did he pass any *serranos*. They were coming home from the market — a man and his wife and their tiny baby. Dusty and ragged they looked beside these cheerfully dressed Indians near the great city — though some of these same lowland Zapotecs had been *serranos* once. Márcos had never seen these very *serranos* before, but he had seen many just like them at home.

As the man trudged past him, Márcos glanced at him out of the corner of his dark eyes. His black, pointed felt hat was pulled 'way down over his ears, and his black hair swirled beneath it. A stubby beard fluffed out from his chin. Under his hat his brown eyes darted hither and thither like those of a *tigre's* at bay, and his skin was darker than most of the other Indians who passed him. One of his trouser legs was rolled up and one was flapping, and inside the rolled-up one was a leg the color of brown rocks and almost as hard.

A little thrill crept up Márcos' spine as he saw the strong muscles of this *serrano* who belonged to his people and his mountains.

Márcos had never seen these very serranos before.

A woman trudged behind the man. She did not wear the dainty dress of the Indians in this pleasant valley. Indeed no! Her hat was half a golden gourd. Her coarse white blouse had long full sleeves, and a close-fitting neck, and it was gray with age and dust. A long slit in the shoulder of her blouse showed the brown skin underneath.

Around her hips was wrapped a heavy woolen skirt that seemed far too warm for such a sunny day, and hanging from her back was a thick gray *serape* in the shape of a little hammock. In this hammock snuggled the tiny baby, just the top of its fuzzy black hair showing.

"They are going back to the stars," thought Márcos a little wistfully, as he turned and stared at them. He felt like joining them and going home.

Then a thought swept over him. "I am going home next year, or in two or three years just before the first rain of the rainy season. I shall drive a pair of oxen before me. My father will be watching for me on the brow of the hill, and my mother will set the mutton stew a-boiling."

He walked stolidly on through this gracious valley, across a bridge of stone which Spaniards had built a long time ago, and up a green hill. And then a little village popped into view.

Márcos stood still and stared. He had never seen a village just like this one before. The houses, thatched with red tiles, were built of adobe all the way through, and the adobe was painted! One house was painted the blue of the river under the swinging bridge. One was painted the yellow of the sun. One was painted the green of new onion blades.

Márcos hurried down the trail into the wider street of the village. This street ran in front of a fence of tall organ cactus that hemmed in the little colored houses. A very nice fence it was. The gate was open, and on a knoll nearest the gate stood a little yellow house.

The boy stepped up to the gate and peered at the yellow house, the red-tiled roof, and jars of gay geraniums in nooks and corners. He stared so long that some one from the house called to him:

"*Pasé!* Come in!"

Márcos felt ashamed and darted away.

"*Pasé!*" The pleasant voice spoke in Spanish.

Márcos knew many Spanish words because a cousin of his father's lived part of the year in the great city, and always returned home when the ground was ready for plowing and seeding. Indeed, this cousin had forgotten almost all of his Zapotec Indian words, and spoke in Spanish most of the time.

Márcos glanced up again at the little yellow house from which the voice had floated. Along a sunny side of the wall ran a roofed-over *corredor* or veranda, and sitting under the roof was an old man. He was smiling at Márcos.

"*Pasé!*" he called again.

Márcos bravely stepped inside the gate and ran up a little rise to the old man's hut. He leaned against the wooden post of the *corredor*.

"*Adiós!*" said the man, smiling.

"*Adiós!*" replied Márcos shyly.

"You see what I am making?" asked the old man proudly.

The boy nodded. The old Indian was sitting on the earth in the midst of small bowls of black clay. Bowls and more bowls were scattered on each side of him, waiting for the sun to dry them enough for the firing. While the boy was watching, the old man picked up a wad of black clay from a thick mass near his hand. He set the clay on flat stone, took up another stone, and pounded the clay until it was as flat and round as a *tortilla*.

Márcos watched him very carefully. Never had he seen clay bowls made this way. His mother always rolled the clay into coils between the palms of her hands, and built up her bowls and *ollas* coil by coil. But this old man was making his dish all in one piece!

"Now watch!" said the bowl-maker. He lightly scooped up the flat, round piece of clay and slapped it over a bowl which he had set upside down on the earth. He shaped the clay carefully around the bowl. Then he picked up a sharp thread of maguey—the wild century plant that sprinkled the hillsides everywhere, and he sliced off the rough edge of the clay just as if he were trimming pie crust. Now it was the size and shape of the other bowl, and he set it on the sunny earth to dry.

Márcos grinned. Well! That was a quick way of making bowls. He would tell his mother about it some day. He picked up a piece of clay near him and pressed it between his fingers. It was a rubbery clay and it could do queer tricks.

The old man pounded another piece of the curious clay, slapped it

over the bowl, and began trimming off the edge with the sharp thread. Ha! The thread snapped in two! He could not finish trimming the bowl!

"This thread has snapped in two!" muttered the old man, half to himself, "and I have no other here."

"I will get you some more," said Márcos. He had seen the graceful blue magueys, with their crinkling leaves, growing on a hillside just behind the village. He ran out of the gate, flew around the cactus fence, and darted up a rocky slope. A gray-blue maguey plant grew from a cluster of rocks in front of him.

Márcos drew from his belt a pocket knife which his father's cousin had given to him, cut off one of the leaves, and scraped off the thick bluish skin. Underneath this skin were long, creamy threads of fibre. He ran down to the little yellow house again, pulled out of the leaf some strong, stout threads, and handed them to the old man.

"Good!" said the bowl-maker. "You are just in time." The edge of the new bowl was sagging a little. He clipped off the rest, and set the bowl on the earth to dry.

Márcos sat down in the *corredor* and pulled and twisted a thread of fibre which he held in his hand.

Good, that fibre. It was strong. It was light. Well he knew that fibre. It could make nets. It had made his own. It could make ropes. It could cut off the ragged edges of clay bowls. There was magic in that thread. There was magic in all thread. Maguey thread, corn-silk thread, goat's hair thread, cotton thread.

Márcos pulled and twisted a thread of fibre.

The old man was watching him curiously.

"You have pointed fingers," he said. "They are even more pointed than mine." He held out his hand and showed Márcos his fingers. "And I am proud of my fingers."

Márcos shyly hid his fingers in the blouse of his jacket. The bowl-maker glanced at the jacket, then,

"What do you carry in your jacket?" he asked. "And what is that in your net?"

"Green apples from the mountains in my net," said Márcos, "and *tortillas* and mutton and bananas in my jacket."

"Stay the night with me," said the old man. "I will give you shelter if I may cook some of your apples for apple sauce. My wife has gone to the faraway market in Tlacolula to sell my bowls, and she will spend the night with her cousin. I shall be alone if you do not stay. And I have no *centavos* for food until she returns."

"I will stay," said Márcos, glad that he would not have to curl outside the cactus fence for the night. Already the grape-colored shadows of late afternoon were creeping across the dusty road. The old man rose and led the way into the kitchen of the little adobe house.

He built a fire of charcoal in the brick stove in the corner, chopped up the apples, and poured them into a clay cooking bowl. Then he sprinkled water and rough, grayish sugar upon them.

Soon the apple sauce was purring, and Márcos was dividing the chunk of mutton, the *tortillas*, and bananas with the old bowl-maker.

As the old man handed Márcos a bowl for the apple sauce he said:

"Keep it. You have done me more than one good turn this day. You fetched me my thread, you divided your supper, and," he chuckled, "you are keeping me from being lonely."

Márcos looked long at the bowl. It had been fired, so it was strong and good. Creamy yellow glaze covered it, and circles of red and green decorated it. The bowl was beautiful.

"Thanks," he said simply, as the old man filled it with sauce from the apples of the boy's own mountain.

"And thanks for the apple sauce," said the old bowl-maker.

VII

The Soup Woman and the Centavos

Early in the morning Márcos was on the road again, his little yellow bowl packed between straw on the top of his apple-net. The road widened now into a dusty highway on which Indians were traveling to some market place beyond.

The women carried baskets of flowers and fruit on their heads. The men carried mats of cocoanut fibre, strings of wooden bird cages and trays of buns. Ox carts creaked slowly by, and little burros pattered along on their dainty feet.

Village after village Márcos passed, but no voice called to him as he peered through the gate, and no one asked him what he carried in his net.

He was too shy to shout, "Apples! Apples!" as the other vendors shouted their wares. He just hoped that someone would see the shining green skins gleaming through holes in the mesh.

He had been traveling most of the morning when he suddenly stopped and stared at the road beneath him. It was different. It was no longer dusty. It was paved in stones — cobble stones like those in the bed of the river under the swinging bridge. Round stones. Polished stones. And before him rose something dreamlike. Was this the great city?

He ran up a little knoll by the side of the cobbled highway and looked down. He gasped with surprise. He ran up a higher knoll and looked down again, and then he ran to a higher knoll still. He sat on this highest knoll with his chin cupped in his hands. He stared.

No, this was not the great city, because his father had told him carefully all about that. This was a very big village, bigger than all the others. It was so big that he would have to go straight through instead of going around it.

He saw a wide river of red-tiled roofs glistening with sun-gold in the noontime. Many of the roofs were furred with green mosses. He saw a creamy church with two bell towers, and a scarlet dome like a red apple set between them.

But the strangest thing Márcos saw in this village was the variety of colors of the painted adobe houses. He did not know there were so many colors in the world. These colors ran through all shades of

He sat on this highest knoll.

the rainbow. A curious thing about them was that many of the houses had colors and colors painted over each other, like the many folds of an onion skin.

Should Márcos peel off the blue paint he would find pink. If he peeled off the pink paint he would find yellow. If he peeled off the yellow paint he would find green. Márcos could see patches of these colors underneath each other. He guessed that the houses had been painted over and over again; and each time they were painted, they were done a different color.

Márcos liked those mixed colors very much. They were like weaving of the finest kind. Threads of one color running crosswise under threads of another color, so that the under shade showed through.

He stared and stared at this village. He saw little twisting streets. Indian women were pacing up and down them, bearing tall water jars on their heads. Indian men were trudging along them, carrying heavy burdens. One old Indian was patching cobbles in the street.

Márcos saw a drove of burros with fluffy cornstalks bristling from their sides, and a boy running up the curving steps of a bell tower.

All these things he saw because he had the far sight of a boy who had lived always in the mountains, and who had gazed from peak to peak since babyhood. He had the eyes of a wild creature, a wild mountain hawk.

From the bell tower clanged the church bells, swung by the hand of the boy who had climbed the steps; and cries of vendors floated up from the streets.

"Surely I can trade my apples in this village," said Márcos to himself, running down the three knolls and joining the crowd in the highway again. His bare toes felt the cobbled street for the first time, though often they had curled around stones on his mountains at home.

He trudged down a hill with flocks of vendors, and found himself in a great, tree-fringed square. Ah! This was the park! Often he had heard his father say that every big village had a park in the middle of it. He sat down on the very edge of a carved bench to rest a little while.

He didn't know whether he was supposed to sit there or not,

though other people were sitting on the benches. A fine Mexican gentleman in strange city clothes of gray was reading a newspaper on one bench. A little Indian woman with a blue *rebozo* over her head and shoulders, and a tiny baby asleep in its folds, rested on another bench. An old Indian man wrapped up in a scarlet *serape* was snoozing on another bench. The air was a sleepy air.

In the center of the park rose a bandstand with a fancy railing. Little paths ran around it and wandered out in all directions. Dark trees like mountain trees were planted among the paths, but they didn't smell like mountain trees. They didn't smell like pines or any other trees that Márcos knew.

Boys and girls darted through the park carrying bangles and other trinkets to sell, and a little bootblack with tiny box and stool ran to the fine gentleman. Márcos was very much surprised to see the gentleman peer over the rim of his newspaper and nod to the bootblack to go ahead. He set one foot on the little stool, and the bootblack opened his box and drew out a brush. It was easy to get that job!

Márcos stole away from his bench and left the park by one of its curving little paths. He stepped into a narrow, cobbled street and let it take him where it would. It ran down a hill a little way between houses of bright colors.

He walked slowly now, staring at the houses on either side of him. Some were low and some were high, and they clung to each other like timid children. All had balconies gay with jars of geraniums and green parrots in cages. A Mexican woman in a frilly pink dress was rocking in a cane chair on one balcony.

"Boy! Boy!" she called, as Márcos wandered down the street. He glanced up and saw her peering down at him, over the railing. "What have you in your net?"

"Apples," replied Márcos, suddenly hanging his head and scratching a cobble with his bare toe.

"How much?"

Márcos glanced over his shoulder at his net. It was only a third full.

"Twenty *centavos*," he replied.

The woman bristled. "Too much. Ten *centavos*."

"Twenty *centavos*," repeated Márcos, walking along slowly.

"No, no. Fifteen *centavos*."

"Twenty!"

"Ten!"

"Twenty!" And Márcos ambled down the street.

"Come back!" cried the woman. "I will give you fifteen!"

Márcos turned back. This was what he was waiting for. When he reached the doorway, his customer was already standing in it. Had she flown down from the balcony, thought Márcos? She was holding out a deep, brown-glazed bowl. Márcos carefully plucked his own little yellow bowl out of his net, and poured the apples into her bowl. They rattled like river water over stones. Now he had nothing left to trade. But he had fifteen *centavos!*

He tied the coppers in a corner of his jacket and trudged up the street again. He was hungry. He had eaten nothing for breakfast because the old bowl-maker's cupboard was empty.

He walked through the park and stepped into a street where many

"Twenty centavos," repeated Márcos.

people were flocking. Soon he found himself at the archway of a great, roofed-over market. He peered inside. It was thronged with Indians swaying like corn leaves in the wind. Their voices rustled like blowing corn leaves, too.

These Indians were dressed like the lowland Zapotecs he had seen on the trail the day before, and the children were dressed just like their parents.

Here and there were Mexican ladies among the Indians, their smooth, black, uncovered hair parted neatly, their silk dresses a-swish, and the heels of their shiny slippers high. Neat little bare-footed Indian maids or sturdy *mozos* or menservants trailed after them, carrying market baskets in the crooks of their arms.

The sharp tang of meat and fresh vegetables and fruits floated to the quivering nose of Márcos, and he stepped into the busy market.

He passed the meat stall. It was sizzling with flies, though he didn't mind that. But how could he use raw meat without his mother to cook it?

He passed the vegetable stall. Fragrant as a wild flower garden in spring, this vegetable stall. Pearly onions and rosy beets and curly squashes. But why should he buy these without his mother to cook them?

He passed the buns — Ah! He started to untie the knot in his jacket. He could buy one of these buns. But just then he smelled a whole feast! At the very back of the market place was a restaurant set up for serving vendors and buyers who had come from far places like himself.

Three women were standing behind a long counter. They were cooking and serving and chatting, too. Many Indians were sitting on a low bench before the counter, eating what these three had cooked.

Márcos perched himself silently on one end of the bench and pointed to a steaming bowl of soup.

One of the three women dished out a foaming bowl of soup and handed it to Márcos. The second woman handed him two *tortillas*, and the third woman a cup of coffee.

Márcos forgot the market and the great city and everything else. He whisked the soup into his mouth with the heavy spoon, sipped the coffee loudly, and set his teeth into a good thick *tortilla*.

He hadn't tasted such a fine meal since he left his mother's hut in the mountains. He held out his bowl for more soup, and then he remembered and drew it back again. This soup woman wasn't his mother. This soup woman and the others would want pay. Already the soup woman's hand was stretched out to his. She seemed to be the head woman.

"How much?" asked Márcos, and how he wished that he had asked, "How much?" first. His heart shook.

"Fifteen *centavos!*" said the woman sharply.

Márcos stared. Fifteen *centavos* for a bowl of soup and two *tortillas* and a cup of coffee!

"Ten!" said he stubbornly.

"Fifteen!"

"Ten!"

"It's ten if you stand up and eat, but fifteen if you sit down," scolded the soup woman.

Márcos' jaw dropped. What difference did that make? Why, he could eat lying down on his back if he had to!

Already the soup woman was chatting with her two companions, as though it didn't matter. But she still held out her hand.

"Come, be quick!" she snapped. "Fifteen!"

Márcos untied the corner of his jacket and handed the woman the fifteen *centavos* he had just earned. He rose from the bench and slipped away in the crowd. He had nothing now. No *centavos*, and no apples to trade.

And then he smiled a merry little smile to himself. "But I've got a good dinner inside of me, anyway!" he chuckled. "And my little yellow bowl."

VIII

The Lady in Lilac

It was a lonely little figure that trudged to the park and sat on the edge of the same bench again. It was the time of the *siesta* — the rest time in the warm part of the day. Shutters of stores were pulled down, wooden blinds of windows were drawn close, and everybody was resting somewhere.

Those who had no cool homes in which to rest were sitting idly on the park benches, or curled in doorways, or nestling in the shade of the church wall. Some of them were even propped up, half dozing, against the great carved doors of the church.

Márcos looked around him with wondering eyes.

Márcos looked about him with wondering eyes. If he were home, now, he would be resting under a tree at the edge of the cornfield. He would be sprawling on the soft brown earth, not sitting up straight on a park bench. The sun would be pouring into his face, and baking his skin a darker brown than ever.

With half shut eyes he watched the scene. One old Indian, on his way to rest somewhere, was kneeling at the fountain, cupping his hands for a drink of water. A click came from across the street, and a slender arm reached out of the window of a pink house and drew the shutters. A brisk little Indian woman trotted home from a morning at the washing tank, a basket of crinkled clothes, sun-dried on the bushes, on her head.

Márcos yawned — a deep wide yawn. He bent his head over his chest. He slept.

Clangity-clang! Clangity-clang! The church bells wakened him with a start. He shook himself and glanced up. The great copper bell in one of the bell towers was waking up from its nap, too. An Indian boy was leaping on the rope, like *el tigre* upon its prey.

The lively, swinging bell, that looked like a huge, upside-down poppy, made little shivers run up and down Márcos' spine. He would rather hear the thunder growl in the mountains, or the waterfall dance down the rock slides, than this jangling thing. He hopped up from his bench and ran down a little side street.

And then he stopped short and laughed.

"If I am going to live in the great city beyond," he said to himself, "I shall have to listen to many strange noises that I have never heard before. Perhaps they will not seem strange to me after a little time."

While he was standing in the middle of the cobbled street laughing to himself, a voice called out from a doorway:

"Boy! Boy!"

Where had he heard that voice? Ah! It was a voice in the little village back there, and it had floated down from a balcony. But this was a kinder voice. It did not have the sharp edge of the other. Márcos shook himself wider awake.

"Boy! Boy! Come here!"

Márcos stepped toward the archway of a pretty, lilac-colored house. In the archway stood a slender, dark-haired woman as pretty as the house. She wore a lilac-colored silk dress and dainty earrings swung from her ears.

"Do you want to water my garden this afternoon?" she asked. "I will give you ten *centavos*. My other boy has gone to a birthday feast."

Márcos stared at her. Water her garden? What did she mean? In the mountains at home the rain watered the cornfield. Only the rain. Could he ask the rain to come before it was time? And why should there be need of watering a garden in the rainy season?

The Mexican woman guessed his thoughts and she smiled.

"Come with me," she said. She led him through the shadowy arch into a flowery *patio* beyond, through a gate in the wall, and into a terraced vegetable garden.

"For three days the thunder shower has not fallen in our village," said she, "and I have young plants set out. They need watering."

She led Márcos down to the first terrace. Tiny radish plants stood in one row. Tiny crisp lettuce plants in another row. Tiny chard plants in another row. They looked wet enough to Márcos, but they didn't look wet enough to her. She wrinkled her brow and glanced at the sky."

"And I do not see a cloud," she said.

Márcos didn't see a cloud, either, but he tasted a warm taste in the air that meant rain. But it wouldn't be polite to tell her so.

"Water these three rows," said the woman in lilac. "Then go down to the second terrace and water the young plants down there — only the young plants, understand. Then go down to the third terrace and water the young plants down there."

She turned and walked lightly toward the gate in the *patio* wall, but Márcos didn't move. Once she glanced back.

"Hurry!" she called, as she saw him standing frozen there. Then her eyes crinkled into a smile. She understood now.

"The water is in a well over there," she said, pointing, "and a water *olla* is lying on the ground beside the well. Sprinkle the water with your hands. Do not pour it upon the plants."

Márcos darted over to the well and peered into it. It was a deep well. Water glistened at the bottom of it. He picked up the black

water *olla*. His eyes grew wide. It was an *olla* from his own village! It was an *olla* of his mother's own making! Perhaps his father had sold this *olla* to this very woman in the market of the great city beyond.

He let the *olla* down into the well with the long rope which was tied around its neck. He watched the rope as it slid down. It was a fine piece of rope woven from the same kind of maguey thread with which the old bowl-maker had trimmed his bowl. Perhaps his own father had made that rope! How strong such little threads could be when they were woven together. Even the swinging bridge had been woven of threads!

Márcos tugged at the rope now. The *olla* was heavy with water. Good and tough that rope! It didn't break with its burden. He pulled up the *olla*, looped up the coils of rope again, rested the *olla* on his hip, and ran between the rows. He sprinkled the young radishes with water, the young lettuce, the young chard.

Then he ran down the steps to the next terrace and sprinkled the young plants down there. Funny! What little rows! Why didn't the woman plant corn? Better the cornfields and the oxen and the plow.

He let the olla down into the well.

And then he stood still and chuckled as he thought of oxen climbing up and down those tiny terraces.

"Keep on watering! Keep on watering!" called a voice from a balcony above, but there was a gay laugh in the voice.

Ah! He had forgotten. It was not his father's cornfield he was watering. He was earning his pay now. He would have to keep busy.

Again and again he ran to the well, let down the *olla*, pulled it up, sprinkled the young plants. Then he felt a warm splash on his cheek. How could the water from the *olla* hop up and sprinkle his cheeks? He heard a growl in the mountains — his mountains. Then he saw a flicker of bright light.

"You have watered enough," called a voice. "It is going to rain."

Márcos glanced up at the balcony just in time to see a lilac skirt whisk into a shadowy room up there.

"She is coming now!" thought Márcos. "She will pay me nothing because it is going to rain and my work has been wasted. Or maybe she will pay me only half. That would be fair. I have not watered all her plants."

Yet he was tired through and through. The constant hurry without rest, the strain of lifting the heavy *olla* out of the well so many times, the chasing from terrace to terrace — these things had tired him after the long tramp of the morning.

The woman in lilac stood in the gateway of the *patio* wall and called him to come. He ran once more to the well, dropped the *olla* gently where he had found it, and stepped quickly towards her. She held a piece of silver and some copper *centavos* in her hand.

"Ten *centavos* I promised you," said she, "and here they are."

Márcos stared. She was going to give it all to him, then? He held out his palm for the five-cent piece and five *centavos*. She let them fall into it. He tied them in a corner of his jacket.

"Thanks," he said, a note of wonder in his voice.

"For nothing," she replied. And then she added kindly: "You did well. I watched you. If I had no boy to water my garden I would take you." But she didn't say out loud that he had a pleasant way with him, and that her boy always wore a scowl. "Where are you going?"

"To the great city."

"What are you going to do there?"

"Find work."

"What kind of work?"

"What I, what I—"

"I know — what you can get," she helped him. And then she put her hand on his shoulder, because she liked this boy, and she said:

"Take what you can get. That is right. But keep your eyes open always for something better. Better! Better!" She smiled.

Márcos' tongue unhooked itself now, and he told her how he wanted to buy a pair of oxen and drive them home to his father in a year or more.

"It will take much more than one year to earn them," said she. "It will take two years, three years maybe, for they cost much money. But put your earned coins in a jar, or slip them under a loose tile, or hide them in a chink of the wall. Save them. And the day will come when you can drive your oxen home. And now, *Adiós*, and good luck!"

"*Adiós*," said Márcos with a smile. He walked through the *patio*, through the shadowy archway, into the cobbled street. The rain drops were gathering. He shook out his rain cape and threw it over his shoulders.

"That woman is a good woman," he thought to himself. "She is better than the soup woman at the restaurant. That soup woman wanted five more *centavos* because I sat down instead of standing up, and this lady gave me five more *centavos* than I have earned. All that money wasted because the thunder shower came!"

He trudged up the street in the dancing rain, hardly knowing where he was going. But soon he found himself on a wide muddy highway leading out of the village into the great city beyond.

As he trotted through the spatter of raindrops, he thought:

"There are too many people and not enough stars, but some of the people are good and some of the people are not so good. I will be careful how I choose my master."

IX

The Old Convent

As Márcos plodded along the highway to the great city of Oax-aca, the rain drove into his face and trickled down the palm ribbons of his rain cape. Shadows of dusk were weaving among the rain drops. But the thunder was growing fainter and fainter, and the lightning flashes were few.

Flocks of Indians crowded beside him, bound to the market in the great city. They were going to spend the night in the city, thought Márcos, so they could be at the market in the earliest dawn.

Where would they sleep? Would they huddle against the closed shutters of the market place? Would they crawl into doorways? Some of them would have friends in the city, but not Márcos. Where would he sleep?

The rain trickled down the palm ribbons of his rain cape.

All these things he thought as he pressed on to the great city. He followed the others. In the dusk he bumped against crates of live chickens, bags of corn, bags of wool, bags of grain. He jounced into turkeys and squealing pigs clutched under arms, and he scraped against the flanks of burros and oxen. The rain drops fell no longer. Dusk, dusk, and more dusk, and then —

He saw the lights of the great city! He saw yellow lights from window slits in walls that looked like strange, dark mountains. He saw flickering torches in the street where a few vendors were selling their wares under roofs. He smelled the smell of many people.

"There are too many people and not enough stars," he muttered to himself. He looked up wildly. He could not see the stars! Instead he saw towering, shadowy walls leaning toward him. He trembled. What if there should be an earthquake! He wished he were home in his little thatched hut. He wanted to be close to the warm earth; he wanted plenty of earth all around him. There was no earth here! Not a square foot of it! Cobbles, cold cobbles under his bare feet!

He swayed along with the crowd. Like a rushing river they all swept around the corner, plunged down a twisting street of cobbles, and one by one were swallowed up in the darkness.

Márcos followed them. He passed the closed shutters of a great market. Through the slits of the shutters he smelled the warm odors of the busy market day that had just passed. He smelled the sweat of many people, the faint perfume of flowers, the ripe skins of bananas, and musty leather of sandals and thongs.

He crossed the street with the rest of the crowd, and was shoved along a wide tiled runway leading up to a great archway. And inside the archway this is what he saw.

He saw a vast courtyard in the middle of great walls hung on all four sides with two balconies, one above the other. In the courtyard was a crush of Indians and oxens and ox carts and burros. By the light of candles and torches and lanterns the men were throwing down hay for their animals, unhitching them from carts, or lifting off their burdens.

Women were feeding their pigs or goats or chickens that they had brought to sell at the market, and sleepy little children were crawling into beds of hay. Up an old stone staircase leading from

He followed the others.

the courtyard, Indian families were wearily trudging to the floors above, their bundles on their backs.

Márcos stood gaping in the midst of all this whirl and flutter. This was a very nice place to spend the night, he thought. Why had his father never told him of this place before? Friendly animals flocking all around him, to squeal or bray or crow, whatever was their nature. He looked up into the sky above the great courtyard. He could see a few stars. Only a few, though, and very faint. Not like the glittering stars at home.

He sat down in a dusky corner and listened to the chatting around him. Everybody was speaking in Spanish. Only now and then he heard an Indian word. If he lived in the city he would have to speak Spanish, too. But he would never forget his Indian language as did his father's cousin.

Chatter, chatter, chatter! Mostly the men were chattering. The women and children were too tired to talk.

"This place is an ex-*convento*," said one. Márcos pricked up his ears. An ex-*convento*! He knew what that was. That was an old-time convent. His father had told him about these old convents in the great city, where nuns used to teach Indian children.

"Yes," said the other. "It is very old. It has not been used for a convent for many years."

"I am going to sleep down here by my burros," said the first man, gathering up a pile of hay, and carrying it to his little animals near by.

"And I am going to the floor above," said the other. And they parted for the night.

Márcos rose softly to his feet. "I am going to sleep above, too," he whispered to himself. "Nearer the stars."

He passed through the crowd in the courtyard and mounted the wide stone steps. Flares lighted the way. In the middle of each step was a hollow place where many footsteps had worn down the stone in years past.

Up and up and up. He was alone on the stairs now. He was alone on the first roofed balcony that ran around the four walls of the ex-*convento*. He peered into tiny rooms that opened off this balcony. In many of the rooms whole families were unrolling their palm sleeping mats, and curling upon them, wrapped in their warm *serapes*.

He tiptoed up another wide staircase. This led him to another balcony without a roof, and to other rooms opening from it. He felt more at home here. He was nearer the stars. He peeked into the little rooms. They were empty.

And then he chose a room for himself. "This is my room," he said softly. "It is my little mountain cave." He stepped into a tiny, plastered cell. This was his room. Just dimly he could see the shadowy, white walls. One tiny, round, barred window pierced one wall. He stood on tiptoe and peered through it. He found one star!

He unrolled his sleeping mat and spread it in a corner. He rolled up his sweetly scented rain cape for a pillow. He lay down.

A clatter and chatter awoke him. It was early morning. Rays of sun peeked through the little round window. He leaped to his feet, ran out on the balcony and peered over the wooden railing.

Burros were braying in the courtyard, pigs were squealing, Indians were bustling around their animals, watering and feeding them. Indians were setting their wares on their heads and trotting off to market. Lowland Zapotec Indians everywhere. Scurrying, flurrying.

Márcos ran back to his little cave, rolled up his mat with his rain cape, and slung them across his back. He threw his *serape* upon his shoulder. He peeked into his net. The yellow bowl in its wrapping of straw was safe.

Then he ran out to the balcony again and stole down the icy-cold stone steps. On the balcony he met many Indian families tumbling out of their rooms like bees out of hives. They carried many wares for the market.

Márcos stole down the last flight of stairs. On the last stone step a hand was laid on his shoulder.

"Where did you sleep last night?" asked a rough voice. Márcos glanced up. A tall man with black whiskers was frowning down upon him. The boy tried to wriggle out of his grasp, but the long fingers clutched his coat sleeve.

There was no use in telling this man that he slept close to the stars in a mountain cave, so he said simply:

"I slept 'way up there," and he pointed with one finger to the upper balcony.

"What for?" he asked the man with the black whiskers.

The man held out his hand, the palm upward. "Ten *centavos*," he said. "You owe me ten *centavos*."

Ten *centavos*! Ten *centavos* for lying down and sleeping? Ten *centavos*? What for?

"What for?" he asked this man with the black whiskers.

"For renting one of my rooms, of course," said the man gruffly, his eyes searching the passing crowd for any who had not paid. "I have to pay rent for this *ex-convento*, and you have to pay me. That's fair, isn't it? I'm not giving my rooms away, am I?"

Márcos couldn't quite understand. At home no stranger was ever left outside in the chill night when he could sleep in the little thatched house of Márcos' parents. And a nice fat supper and breakfast he was given, besides. Márcos wondered.

"Come, come, come!" growled the man, staring now at the tied-up corner of the boy's jacket. "Give me ten *centavos*!"

Márcos slowly untied the corner of his jacket. He handed the man the precious silver piece and the copper *centavos* which the woman in lilac had given to him for watering a garden that didn't need watering. The man with the whiskers closed his fingers over the coins and walked away.

Márcos stood staring after him for a long time. His ten *centavos*! His breakfast. And then he suddenly felt dizzy. He almost swayed as he stood there in the bustle of Indians, in the warm smell of animals, and the whiffs of breakfast which the Indians were eating.

He was puzzled. He was hungry. He was lonesome — very, very lonesome. He wished he could hear his mother patting the good *tortillas* for breakfast. He wished she was folding one *tortilla* over a piece of mutton and handing it to him. He wished he could eat his own breakfast, too.

But no, no! He had to pay ten *centavos* for lying down and going to sleep. He couldn't quite understand. He couldn't quite understand this great city — yet.

X

The Great City

Márcos stood in the twisting cobbled street outside the market place. He was peering through the great doorway from which the shutters had been lifted. He dared not to go into that buzzing place. Of a truth there were too many people and not enough stars.

It was very much like the market in the village of the woman in lilac, only larger, much larger. Great stalls were piled high with golden mangoes, purple plums, and pineapples. They overflowed with frilly, green vegetables and fragrant flowers.

High wide racks were hung with bright cotton scarves and belts and aprons. There were racks with ropes and leather sandals and saddle packs of cocoanut fibre; racks with ribs of beef and shoulders of lamb, and sausages.

Soon, tomorrow perhaps, Márcos felt he might venture into the market. But now, such a hollow feeling hid under his red cotton sash that he could think of nothing else. How could he earn his breakfast? How? No one in the market needed help. They were all busily doing everything for themselves. He would stroll about the big city and keep his eyes wide open every minute. Perhaps he could find another garden to water.

He trudged past the busy market place and entered a little park. Ah! There was a little old Mexican gentleman snoozing on a bench. He was the only one in the park this busy, bustling morning. If Márcos had only a shoe-shining box and a stool now, he would run up to the old man, speak to him gently, and ask if he wanted his shoes shined. But he didn't have a box and stool.

Slowly Márcos wandered through the park, his eyes staring at everything. He stooped over the rim of a fountain. He cupped his hands and drank. The water was cool and sweet — almost as sweet as mountain water. He pretended that it was food, too.

He walked through the trees to the end of the park. He stared at the great green walls of buildings that rose around it, walls that looked like the cliffs rising above the swinging bridge of vines. They seemed to be rocking. He stared at the carved iron balconies jutting out from them. He wouldn't want to stand on one of those balconies. They didn't look strong enough to hold him. Ah! He didn't know how strong they were! He stared at the great carved doors flung back against the walls.

So, looking this way and that, he presently found himself on a little cobbled street running down a hill. Márcos liked this street. It looked like the street of the woman in lilac. Maybe, good luck was hiding somewhere on this street. He strolled slowly down it, peering into archways.

The low houses of this street were painted in many colors. Some were lilac, like the house of the woman in lilac. Some were creamy yellow. Some were the green of vines with the sun shining through them. None of them were as dark as pine needles. They were all light, light. Low balconies hung over his head and iron-barred windows pierced the walls.

Archways ran straight through the houses, cutting them in two. Beyond the archways glimmered flowery *patios*. In the *patios* Márcos could see lemon trees and banana trees and bright blossoms which he

did not know. Children played by the fountains and hens scratched in the corners.

A little woman in a white blouse and starched pink skirt threw a bucket of soapy water out of an archway. It splashed against Márcos' shoulder. He looked up in surprise, but the little woman had whisked away. She had not even seen him.

Parrots in wooden cages screeched at him as he passed, and two green parakeets played in a sunny spot on a doorstep.

It was a nice street, a homely, cheerful, little street. But everyone in it was busy, going about his own affairs. All belonged there; they were at home. Only Márcos, the little boy from the mountains, did not belong there. No one paid any attention to him.

Only Márcos did not belong there.

It made him feel very homesick. It came over him with a hollow feeling, right down to his toes, that he was all alone in this city of busy happy people. There was no one here to whom he belonged, no one who would turn and say: "Why, there is Márcos! How is Márcos this morning?"

So he left the little gay street, the busy women and the children and the chattering parrots, the bright houses and green vines. He turned his back on them all and set off once more towards the market place.

How did one find work? What did one do when one was small and alone and wanted to find work, work that would help to buy oxen and a plow? How did one set about it, when one knew nobody at all in this big city?

One asked.

All day Márcos wandered up and down the streets. Whenever he saw a place where people were working, where it looked as if they might be glad of a little boy to help them, he stopped and asked. But for all his asking, there would be only a shake of the head. He helped one man to carry baskets of fruit and vegetables from a cart into his shop, and the man gave him a banana. But when all the baskets were carried, and the banana was eaten, then there was nothing more to do there.

Some of the people listened to him before they shook their heads. Some were too busy even to listen. They told him to run along, and not to stand about there, getting in their way. One man said that Márcos had better go back to his own village. Perhaps he might find work there.

By midday Márcos was tired and very hungry. The banana had helped, but it was only a banana. He felt very empty about his middle, and his feet ached from trudging to and fro over the hard stones.

He took a drink from a fountain in the street, and then he sat down on the steps of a big church. It was cool here and shady. He watched the people going back and forth.

So many people. Such a big city! And nowhere, in all these busy streets, was any work for a little boy who wanted to earn his food.

But here at least he could be quiet. There was no one to jostle him, to push him out of the way. He laid his head on his arms, and presently he fell fast asleep.

XI

Márcos Finds a Master

He woke with a great noise in his ears. Ding, dong—ding, dong! For a moment Márcos was very startled. Then he knew that it was the sound of the great bell in the tower above him, like the bell that had wakened him once before, in the village of the woman in lilac. But this time the bell did not frighten him. It seemed to be talking.

"Márcos, Márcos," it seemed to say. "Wake up, Márcos!"

Now there were many more people in the street. Women in fine dresses, peasant women with shawls. Márcos drew back behind one of the big pillars and watched them going by.

The shadows across the street had grown longer. They reached almost across to the opposite walls. It must be nearly sunset, Márcos thought. Sunset, and he had not yet found work to do, or even food to eat.

He passed again by the big market. It was emptying, now. People were packing up their things, getting their carts ready to drive home. No work there.

Through one street after another Márcos went. He would walk and walk, he thought, and then later when it was quite dark he would creep back to the church steps and there, in the shadow of the big pillars, he would curl up, very small so that no one would see him, and perhaps he could sleep there till morning. And tomorrow — who knew — tomorrow he would surely find work.

There was only that empty ache, like a mouse gnawing under his belt, that began to trouble him more and more. If only he could be sitting down, right now, to a good hot meal in his mother's house!

Not even troubling which way he went, jostled by the hurrying people about him, lost and lonely among the clatter of so many strange feet, Márcos wandered on. And presently he turned a corner.

There he was, back in the little cobbled street with the bright houses and the gardens. It looked friendly, as a place does that one has seen before. It was almost like coming home.

There he was, back in the little cobbled street.

There were the arched doorways and the gardens behind them. And there was the same parrot he had seen that morning, drowsy now and sitting all bunched up on its perch.

Slowly, almost on tiptoe, Márcos walked along. Suddenly he stopped short by the archway of a yellow house. He had heard a click-click, from a room somewhere behind the walls. The sound was smothered, as though it came from a cave like his little cave in the *ex-convento*, but Márcos knew that click well. No other ears but the ears of a wild mountain boy could have heard it.

He peered into the archway. Home-made benches lined either side and gay potted geraniums bloomed on the benches. Soft worn tiles lay underfoot, leading on and on . . .

Márcos took one step inside the arch. He listened. The clicking sound grew a little nearer. He tiptoed through the arch and peered into the *patio*. Golden balls hung from an orange tree. Banana leaves rustled in a corner. Lemons hung from a lemon tree.

But Márcos scarcely looked at the trees. For something else had caught his eye. On a cord stretched from lemon tree to orange tree hung threads. Wet threads—wet from the dyeing. Scarlet threads, golden threads, olive threads, purple threads! Threads as soft as corn silk, or the hair of the little kid at the charcoal burner's. Strong as the vines of the swinging bridge!

Márcos stepped across the *patio* and lifted a thread between his fingers. It was cotton thread from tree cotton, he knew that. And the dyes were from mountain plants. He knew that, too.

Then he heard that clicking sound again. Click, click! He peered into a doorway. For just one little moment he could see nothing in the room beyond. It was dusky in there. Then he saw an old wooden loom in one corner, a weaver behind it; and another loom in another corner, a weaver behind it; and another loom and another weaver in another corner. And in the middle of the room, in a patch of late sunlight, he saw a spinning wheel with no one behind it. The stool was empty.

As he stood there, peering into the room, one of the looms stopped clicking. A slender Indian with curling black whiskers slipped off a stool and came towards him.

"What do you want, my son?" he asked in a friendly voice.

Márcos started to move away, but the master of the weaving house touched his arm.

"What do you want?" he asked again. "Are you looking for some-one?"

What could Márcos say? He stood there tongue-tied. Just then the whiff of savory soup from a kitchen beyond reached his nose and he almost said: "I want supper." But hungry as he was, the words of the old goatherd came back to him just in time. "Do not be a beggar."

"I want work," said Márcos, and without knowing it his eyes fell on the empty stool before the spinning wheel.

"Ah," said the weaver, putting a pointed finger to his lips as though he were thinking. Márcos looked at that pointed finger. Then he looked at his own fingers. They were just as pointed as the weaver's.

"I might use a boy like you," said the weaver at last. "He could run my errands, and fetch and carry for my workers. But he must not be afraid of work."

"I am not afraid of work," said Márcos.

"Can you spin?" asked the master.

"I cannot spin—yet," said Márcos, "but I can learn."

"Hm-hm-hm!" hummed the weaver. He stared at the empty stool a long moment.

"My spinner has gone back to the mountains," he said. "His brother was killed in a fall from a horse, and he had to take his place. He has no father. He was a *serrano,* too."

Márcos was silent for a while. Then he asked slowly:

"How long would it take for a spinner to earn a pair of oxen and a plow, after he had learned to spin?"

"Oh, maybe three years, once he had learned," said the weaver thoughtfully. "But I would send him to school while he was spinning my threads, and every rainy season I would let him go back into the mountains, for a little while, to help with the plowing and sowing. And after three years, if he worked hard, I would teach him to be a weaver."

"I will learn!" cried Márcos in a clear voice, and the clicking of the other two looms suddenly stopped. "I will spin your threads for three years, and after three years I will drive my oxen home and then I will come back. For I would rather be a weaver than anything else in the world!"

And suddenly all the threads that Márcos loved — the corn silk thread, the tough maguey thread, the cotton thread and all the others — seemed to weave themselves into a fine gay blanket. Then the blanket swayed before his eyes and he fell back.

The strong arm of the master caught him.

"The boy is faint with hunger," he cried to one of the other weavers. "Run! Tell the *señora* to bring hot soup and *tortillas.*"

"Stay you, stay you," he said gently to Márcos, who was bravely trying to stand. "Sit down here."

He led the boy to the empty stool. Márcos sat down upon it, and it was empty no longer.

"This will be your place," said the weaver kindly. "You shall run my errands and learn to be my spinner of threads."

Late that evening Márcos stood at the workshop door. He had drunk the hot soup and eaten the *tortillas,* and the good food felt comforting in his stomach. In the room behind him the looms were silent; the workers had gone home, but he could hear the plump *señora* moving about, preparing the little bed where he, Márcos, would sleep that night and for many nights to come.

The little street was quiet. The *patio* was quiet. The trees threw clear black shadows on the white stones, and in the dark velvet sky above the stars gleamed softly. Márcos threw back his head to look up at them, smiling.

"I have chosen well," he said to himself. "I have found a good master. There are not too many people here, and just enough stars. I know."